DARTH MAUL'S MISSION

BY ACE LANDERS   ILLUSTRATED BY DAVID WHITE

ISBN 978-0-545-30441-2

LEGO, THE LEGO LOGO, THE BRICK AND KNOB CONFIGURATIONS AND THE MINIFIGURE ARE TRADEMARKS OF THE LEGO GROUP. © 2011 THE LEGO GROUP. PRODUCED BY SCHOLASTIC INC. UNDER LICENSE FROM THE LEGO GROUP.

©2011 LUCASFILM LTD. & TM. ALL RIGHTS RESERVED. USE UNDER AUTHORIZATION.

PUBLISHED BY SCHOLASTIC INC. SCHOLASTIC AND ASSOCIATED LOGOS ARE TRADEMARKS AND/OR REGISTERED TRADEMARKS OF SCHOLASTIC INC.

20   17 18 19/0

PRINTED IN THE U.S.A.   40

FIRST PRINTING, AUGUST 2011

SCHOLASTIC INC.

NEW YORK   TORONTO   LONDON   AUCKLAND   SYDNEY   MEXICO CITY   NEW DELHI   HONG KONG

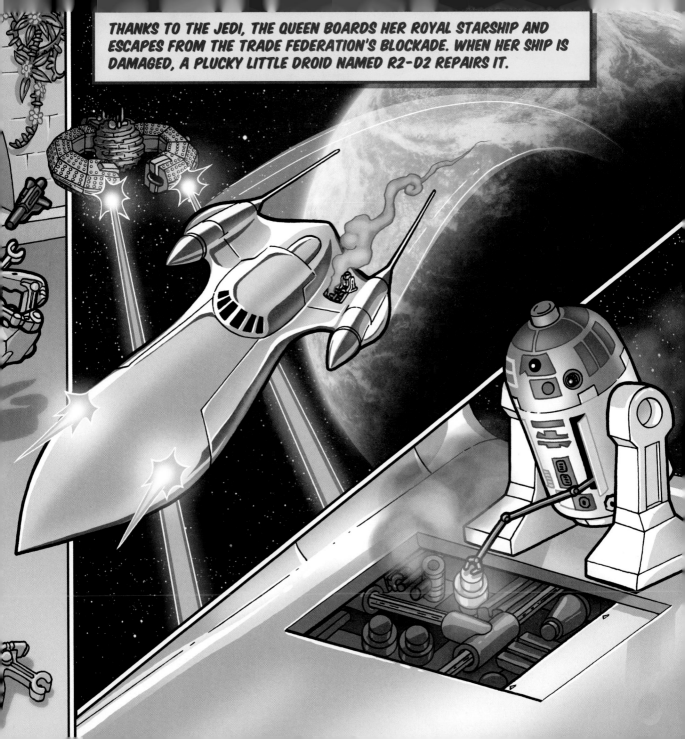

THANKS TO THE JEDI, THE QUEEN BOARDS HER ROYAL STARSHIP AND ESCAPES FROM THE TRADE FEDERATION'S BLOCKADE. WHEN HER SHIP IS DAMAGED, A PLUCKY LITTLE DROID NAMED R2-D2 REPAIRS IT.

WHEN QUI-GON AND HIS TEAM GET BACK TO THEIR SHIP, THEY FIND A STRANGE SIGHT — DARTH MAUI'S PARTY TOWN.

DARTH MAUL AND QUI-GON CLASH, DODGE, AND SLASH AT EACH OTHER. THE SOUNDS OF STRIKING LIGHTSABERS SLICE THROUGH THE DESERT AIR.

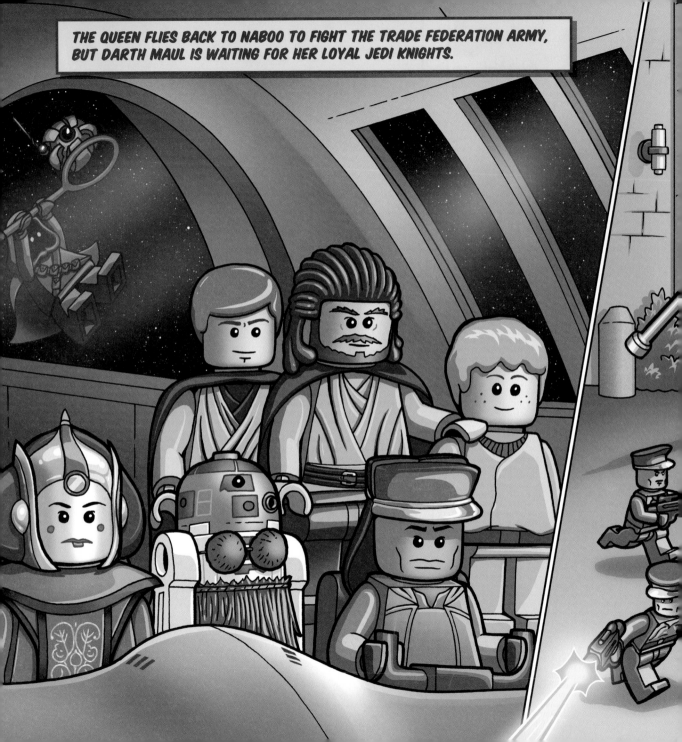

THE QUEEN FLIES BACK TO NABOO TO FIGHT THE TRADE FEDERATION ARMY, BUT DARTH MAUL IS WAITING FOR HER LOYAL JEDI KNIGHTS.

QUI-GON AND OBI-WAN BOTH ATTACK DARTH MAUL. TWISTING AND FLIPPING THROUGHOUT THE FIGHT, MAUL GIVES OBI-WAN A ROUNDHOUSE KICK AND KNOCKS HIM DOWN. THEN HE KNOCKS QUI-GON INTO A CLOSET, SO HE CAN FIGHT OBI-WAN ONE-ON-ONE.

LOCK

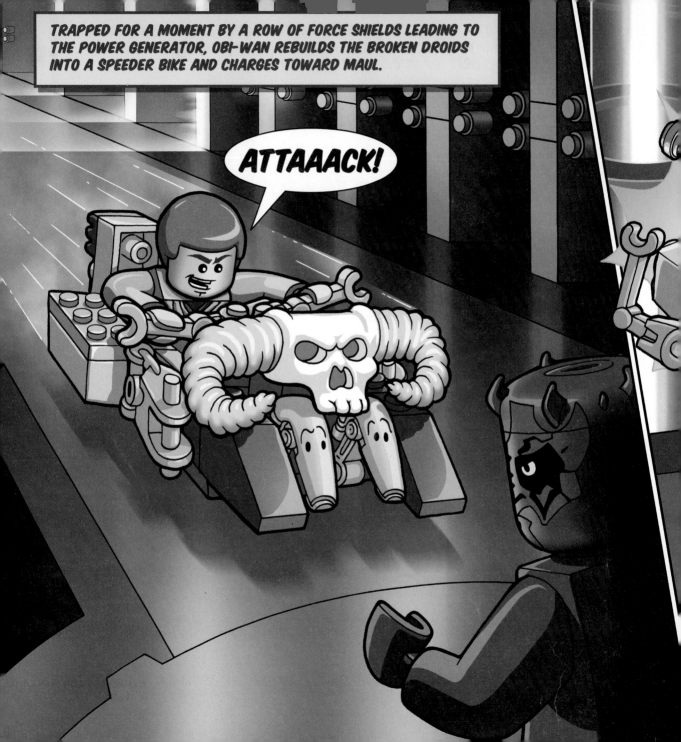

AND FINALLY THE HEROES CAN PARTY.